KIDS CAN'T STOP READING
THE CHOOSE YOUR
OWN ADVENTURE® STORIES!

"Choose Your Own Adventure is the best thing that has come along since books themselves."
—Alysha Beyer, age 11

"I didn't read much before, but now I read my Choose Your Own Adventure books almost every night."
—Chris Brogan, age 13

"I love the control I have over what happens next."
—Kosta Efstathiou, age 17

"Choose Your Own Adventure books are so much fun to read and collect—I want them all!"
—Brendan Davin, age 11

And teachers like this series, too:
"We have read and reread, worn thin, loved, loaned, bought for others, and donated to school libraries our Choose Your Own Adventure books."

CHOOSE YOUR OWN ADVENTURE®—
AND MAKE READING MORE FUN!

Bantam Books in the Choose Your Own Adventure* Series
Ask your bookseller for the books you have missed.

EXILED TO EARTH

BY R.A. MONTGOMERY

ILLUSTRATED BY FRANK BOLLE

BANTAM BOOKS
NEW YORK • TORONTO • LONDON • SYDNEY • AUCKLAND

RL 4, IL age 10 and up

EXILED TO EARTH

A Bantam Book / January 1989

CHOOSE YOUR OWN ADVENTURE® is a registered trademark of
Bantam Books, a division of Bantam Doubleday Dell Publishing Group, Inc.
Registered in U.S. Patent and Trademark Office and elsewhere.

Original conception of Edward Packard

Cover art by Victoria Lisi
Interior illustrations by Frank Bolle

ISBN 0-553-27651-4

Published simultaneously in the United States and Canada

Bantam Books are published by Bantam Books, a division of Bantam Doubleday
Dell Publishing Group, Inc. Its trademark, consisting of the words "Bantam
Books" and the portrayal of a rooster, is Registered in U.S. Patent and Trademark
Office and in other countries. Marca Registrada. Bantam Books, Inc., 666 Fifth
Avenue, New York, New York 10103.

PRINTED IN THE UNITED STATES OF AMERICA

O   0 9 8 7 6 5 4 3 2

WARNING!!!

Do not read this book straight through from beginning to end. These pages contain many different adventures that you may have as a native of the planet Orca. From time to time as you read along, you will be asked to make a choice. Your choice may lead to success or disaster!

Each adventure you take is the result of your choice. You are responsible because you choose. After you make a choice, follow the instructions to see what happens to you next.

Think carefully before you make a decision. You and your best friend Og have been warned not to enter the Lost Region, a forbidden zone full of unknown dangers. You may wind up on an interplanetary spacecraft headed for Earth!

Good Luck!

You and your best friend Og are in the Way Far Back, a patch of wilderness on the planet Orca. Orca's environment is similar to Earth's, but its civilization is much more advanced.

And even an advanced civilization can become dull, especially for a young Orcan like yourself. You and Og were curious. So, despite warnings from the planet's elders, you began to explore the Way Far Back wilderness. Now you and Og are hiking in the direction of the Lost Region, a forbidden zone full of unknown dangers.

You reach the border of the Lost Region and then follow a path almost completely overgrown with dense vegetation.

Turn to page 6.

2

After you and Og are secured in your seats, you pull back the throttle of the spaceship. The ship begins to rumble. Then it lifts off the ground!

"Pull the throttle back farther! Let's zoom out of here!" Og yells.

"I don't want to give it too much juice," you shout over the rumble. "This thing's pretty old. I don't know if it can take the extra power."

You and Og begin to gain altitude. You hover over the fort, then slowly begin to fly in the direction of the Way Far Back and civilization.

"Hey, this runs pretty smoothly for an old bucket of rust," you say as the spaceship glides over the trees toward the coast.

"It sure does," Og agrees. "Give it a little more power. Let's see what it can do!"

You push the throttle forward, and the spaceship levels out and picks up speed. Within seconds you've passed Mach 1. You and Og howl with laughter.

Suddenly the ship starts to vibrate badly. The throttle barely responds when you pull on it. You lose altitude rapidly. Ahead you see the coastline and the sea. You and Og both yank on the throttle and desperately try to guide the spaceship back to land.

"We're not going to make it," screams Og.

Turn to page 12.

"Follow my lead," you mumble to Og, then you start to walk toward the LSAV-3—one of the coast guard's smaller land-sea-air vehicles—parked up the beach. As you near the vehicle, you stop and turn to the captain behind you.

"Excuse me, Captain," you say. "But is that a two-headed sand crab laying eggs on the front seat of your LSAV?"

Two-headed sand crabs are not common on Orca, and the captain and his men move past you for a look.

You and Og take off running.

At a place where the beach curves, you race behind a sand dune. Moments later the beach patrol races past. Trying not to laugh too loudly, you sit down to catch your breath.

Suddenly you're being sucked into the sand. You and Og are in a sand-crab trap! And at the bottom are hundreds of two-headed sand crabs snapping at you with their claws!

You both yell for help and fight furiously to keep from falling deeper into the pit.

Fortunately the beach patrol is still nearby and hears your screams. They rescue you just in time.

"You two mischiefmakers are going to see the elders whether you like it or not," says the captain, wiping the sweat from his brow. "And no more funny business, or we'll toss you both back into that sand-crab pit."

Turn to page 8.

You and Og are awakened at dawn the next morning by a strange humming sound coming from one of the spaceships. The two of you slowly approach the ship, then step inside. There, the humming is louder.

"This looks like an old-fashioned throttle lever," Og says. "On the old spaceships, you gained altitude by pulling on it." Og gives the throttle a light yank, and the spaceship quivers slightly.

Moments later the spaceship stops humming. "It must run on solar energy," you say. "When the sun shines on the solar pods it activates the spaceship's systems." The spaceship starts humming again. "I guess the elders forgot to deactivate it," you say as the humming grows louder.

Turn to page 10.

6

After several minutes, you come to a swirling river.

"Should we swim it?" Og looks at you apprehensively.

"The current looks pretty strong," you say after watching the swirling river rapidly carry a log downstream. "I've also heard rumors that some of the rivers in the Lost Region are infested with Orcan-eating green fish."

You and Og see some logs on the riverbank and decide to make a raft to cross the river. You cut sturdy vines from a Juwawa tree to tie the logs together.

As you lift the end of one log, a large eyeball pops open and stares at you. You're trying to lift an Orcan crocodile!

You drop it quickly and run.

Turn to page 11.

Later, after you've secured your spacecraft to prevent anyone from entering or damaging it out of curiosity, you and Og travel across the Chinese countryside. It's a long journey on narrow, unpaved roads. You travel through farmland and small towns. The people are poor, but industrious, and their mood is one of hope.

Finally, you arrive at an ancient city with many palaces, gardens, and beautiful woodwork. As you enter the city, you experience a feeling of harmony and well-being.

"Welcome! We are glad that you came," your guide tells you. "Many of our leaders will come to talk with you. You may stay here as our guests for as long as you wish. Stay in peace."

You and Og exchange glances. You both know you'll stay as long as necessary, but then you plan to move on. There are a lot more governments on Earth, and now you're curious to meet with them all.

The End

The captain of the beach patrol marches you and Og into the Senate building. He leaves you in a waiting room while he reports to the elders. Twenty minutes later he comes back.

"It's your turn, now," he says with a big smile.

You and Og stand at the open doorway to the chamber of the elders. The Supreme Orcan Senate sits behind an oval table made of volcanic glass. The leader speaks.

"Enter!" she commands. You and Og walk silently into the room.

"We, the Supreme Senate, feel that you two are slaves to your curiosity. And curiosity can often get you into dangerous situations. If you agree to give up your curiosity and behave as do normal Orcans, you are free to resume your lives in Orcan society."

You and Og glance at each other. You imagine Og thinking the same thing you are: If you agree to give up your curiosity, you won't be able to visit the Way Far Back again.

But if you don't agree—what will happen?

If you agree to give up your curiosity, turn to page 18.

If you refuse to give up your curiosity, turn to page 41.

"Do you think it can still fly?" asks Og.

You've been wondering the same thing—and whether you should try to start the spaceship. If the ship won't start and you can't fly out of Fort Triumphant, you may have to face the giant warthogs again.

On the other hand, if the ship does fly, it may break down in flight because it's so old, and you could crash back to Orca.

If you try to leave Fort Triumphant the way you came in, turn to page 14.

If you try to start the spaceship to fly out, turn to page 2.

You and Og scramble up the nearest Juwawa tree and barely escape the crocodile's snapping jaws. You wait in the tree until the crocodile slithers off back into the river.

From your perch in the Juwawa tree you and Og notice some fruit hanging from the upper branches. The Juwawa mango is delicious, and you're both starving! You climb to the top of the tree and pick the fruit.

As you lean forward to pick another mango, you see in the distance four black walls rising out of a clearing in the jungle. You and Og eat the delicious fruit, then decide to hike in the direction of the black walls and explore the area.

Forty-five minutes later you and Og are standing in the clearing. The black walls are mysterious and foreboding. A sign warns: Trespassers Keep Out. But you and Og are too curious to pay attention to a sign. You must find out what's hidden behind the black walls.

Turn to page 21.

The ship skims over the water and comes to a stop. It's still in one place, and so are you. But the spaceship is sinking rapidly. You and Og quickly escape and swim to shore.

When you reach the shore, a beach patrol of the Orcan Coast Guard is waiting for you.

"We think you'd better come with us to see the elders," says the captain of the beach patrol.

If you go before the elders of the Supreme Orcan Senate, they might find out that you were trespassing in the Lost Region, a forbidden zone, and you could get into real trouble. On the other hand, the elders must have been young once themselves. Maybe you should chance their remembering.

If you try to make a run for it,
turn to page 3.

If you decide to go with the beach patrol,
turn to page 8.

14

You and Og close the hatch on the spaceship and go back through the tunnel to the big, wooden door that you came through when you entered Fort Triumphant. You crack open the door and peer outside. Several sleeping giant warthogs wake up. They jump up and wait for you to come through the door.

You and Og quickly gather up some of the loose rocks in the tunnel and begin to throw them at the warthogs. Suddenly they all run away.

"Those warthogs aren't so tough after all," you say to Og as the two of you walk out the door.

"They knew not to give us any trouble," replies Og confidently.

Then you hear a soft rasping sound. You turn, and see an eight-foot, six-legged lizard slithering rapidly in your direction.

Turn to page 42.

Since war ended on Orca light-years ago, the only space warships you've ever seen are those in Orcan history books.

You and Og explore the old fort and the warships as Orca's sun sets in the east. You discover an old monolith overgrown with vegetation. You and Og clear it off and read the inscription: Fort Triumphant.

You remember from your history books that Triumphant was the last of the space forts that guarded Orca from hostile enemies. As sophisticated defense systems were invented, the old forts became obsolete and were torn down.

Fort Triumphant, though, had been preserved as a monument to Orcans who had lost their lives in the space wars. But after light-years had passed, the elders felt even the memory of the space wars was too painful. And Fort Triumphant had been abandoned to rot in the jungle of the Lost Region.

You decide to camp out in the fort overnight and explore it in the morning.

Turn to page 5.

"Our chances of exploring Earth will probably be better if we just go unofficially," you say. "Okay with you, Og?"

Og hesitates, then agrees.

Much later, you and Og are on an interplanetary spacecraft headed for Earth. You're the only life-forms aboard.

"It'll be okay, Og. You'll see. We'll blend right in."

"Oh, sure. We'll blend right in, you say. Did you ever take a look at yourself in a mirror?"

"Come on, Og. Of course I have."

"Well, Earthlings aren't exactly walking around dressed in bright, silver space suits with space helmets. At least not according to the satellite pictures we have of them."

"You're right! I forgot."

"So, how are you going to blend in?"

"We'll fake it," you reply. "Besides the elders must have foreseen this problem. Let's see what kind of costumes they've put aboard."

Turn to page 30.

"Oh, Venerable Ones," you say. "I do hereby fully relinquish my curiosity."

Og makes a similar speech.

The elders survey the two of you with benevolent smiles. They don't speak for several minutes. Then the oldest member addresses you.

"You speak, but I hear no conviction in your words," he says. "You are so young, and have so much to learn. I believe that one day you will have much to give to Orcan society. You are brave, resourceful, and bright. A few years on the planet Earth will do you good."

"A few years down *there*!" you say with a gasp. You exchange an unbelieving glance with Og.

"It is not so very long," the elder says. "Who knows? Perhaps you two can be of use down there. The Earthlings certainly need help."

Turn to page 25.

You and Og are led out of the great hall and taken to a diplomatic courier vehicle. It's a large, silvery, bowl-shaped craft about the size of a typical Orcan house, or a football field on Earth. Rows of viewing ports encircle it.

You and Og are the only ones on board. The craft is preprogrammed. You'll be able to control the ultimate landing site once the craft is in the Earth's atmosphere, but any other attempt to alter the flight plan will destroy the craft.

Turn to page 40.

As you approach the nearest wall you hear a rustling in the bushes. You turn quickly. Out of the bushes dash three giant warthogs. You and Og try to run back into the jungle, but your escape is blocked by more giant warthogs heading in your direction. You turn again and run back toward the black walls, looking for some way to escape.

Turn to page 26.

"Yes. I was in Fort Triumphant, Venerable One," you tell the Supreme Senate leader.

All the elders in the chamber gasp.

The leader shakes her head. Then she continues. "Were you alone?" she asks.

You don't want to lie, yet you don't want to involve Og in whatever punishment is in store for you.

"I'm waiting for your answer," the elder says.

If you protect Og, turn to page 36.

*If you admit that Og was with you,
           turn to page 54.*

"No," says the grinning leader.

"We use these to fly in. Watch, I'll demonstrate." You quickly enter the spaceship with Og before the guerrilla leader has time to react.

You fly safely away from the area and the warlike guerrillas.

"Og," you say, "that's one culture I'm not too curious about."

"Me, neither," Og agrees as the two of you check the computer library on Earth history, searching for another place to land.

The End

Though the elders don't suspect it, you're excited by the chance to go to the planet Earth—the planet of curiosity. Your youth won't be wasted there, you think.

"Now, you two will be Orcan ambassadors," the leader of the Supreme Senate says. "I warn you, it will not be a picnic. We have sent many ambassadors to Earth over the last thirteen thousand years."

"What happened?" you ask. "Did the Earthlings welcome them?"

"Not exactly," the leader replies mysteriously.

You wonder what she means by that, but you know better than to let your curiosity show by asking.

"How are we to be introduced to Earth?" Og wants to know. "Will they believe we are who we say we are?"

"You can carry diplomatic documents and approach one of the major governments. Or," one of the senators explains, "if you wish you can go to Earth as what you are—young adventurers. You would be ambassadors in disguise, as it were."

You and Og briefly discuss your options.

If you want to be formally introduced to one of Earth's governments, turn to page 38.

If you want to go to Earth as an adventurer, turn to page 16.

Og spots an old door with a large rusty lock. You pull on the door, but the lock holds fast. The giant warthogs are nearly upon you. They're so close you can see every hairy wart on the surface of their skins.

You pick up a rock and bash the lock. It breaks off. Quickly you enter through the door and pull it shut, just in time to prevent the warthogs' razorlike tusks from carving you up.

After you and Og catch your breath, you walk through a short, rock-strewn tunnel that comes out into a sunlit courtyard.

"Look!" cries Og in astonishment.

At first the courtyard looks like an ordinary junkyard. But then you see that it's filled with old space warships! They're scattered everywhere!

Turn to page 15.

"Let's go, Og," you say, activating the descender beam. "Everyone is here to greet us." A ray of soft purple light stretches from your ship to the ground. The crowd utters an amazed "Ohhh!"

You and Og begin your descent. But you never reach the ground.

Turn to page 58.

You are given an envelope with the official Orcan seal of peace and a round box containing a gift for the Earthlings. "Well, you're off now," one of the senators says. "Good luck, and don't worry too much about the ones who never came back. The Senate has confidence that you will succeed."

"The ones that never came back?" You and Og look at each other. What has your curiosity gotten you into this time? you wonder.

Turn to page 19.

You and Og disengage your seat restraints. After checking your instrument panel to make sure the atmospheric conditions inside the ship have adjusted to deep-space conditions, you remove your space suits.

A quick search of the spaceship reveals a storage closet full of Earthling-style clothing.

"They all look the same to me," you say, reviewing sample costumes from the many Earth cultures. "Oh, well, let's see what we look like." You and Og start trying on different articles of clothing.

Finally you decide on blue jeans and sweaters. The computer informs you that young people all over Earth wear this costume.

As you're about to close the storage closet, you spot a small, round box. You open it, and then hand it to Og. "Let's take this with us," you say. "It might come in handy as a gift to the Earthlings."

Turn to page 40.

"I don't know," you say as you describe the creature to the computer, and watch the screen for a reply.

A HARMLESS LIFE-FORM ON EARTH.
A NONHOSTILE ENTITY CALLED A CAT.

A red warning light blinks on the computer console and another message appears on the display.

MORE ALIEN LIFE-FORMS
APPROACHING CRAFT.

The computer then asks you for instructions. You begin to comply, but the computer malfunctions, and the spaceship leaves Earth in a surge of power. Unable to correct the malfunction, you and Og glide through space. There's nothing you can do except wait—and hope you'll be rescued. You wonder if your supplies will last.

The End

Your spaceship hovers above the landing field as you and Og prepare to disembark via the descender beam.

When you're standing on Earth, you find yourselves facing a group of military people armed with archaic weapons. An officer steps forward, extending his hand in what is apparently a welcome signal.

Og grabs you by the arm. "Don't trust them! I've got a bad feeling. Let's get out of here," he says.

If you agree with Og's feeling, turn to page 44.

If you ignore Og's plea, turn to page 67.

"We accept your beautiful token of friendship," the Chinese leader says. "It is a good sign that you have chosen a crystal. We believe that the clarity of a crystal predicts the future."

The officer bows slightly, speaks to his aides, and then addresses you.

"China is an ancient culture. We have long recognized the changing seasons, the progress from childhood to old age, the rise and fall of nations. Perhaps you can help this world in its great cycle."

"We'll try," you say.

Turn to page 7.

"No, I didn't enter the Lost Region," you say. As you utter this lie, images of Fort Triumphant flash through your mind. The abandoned spaceships and war artifacts still intrigue you.

You no longer feel intimidated by the Supreme Senate. You take a deep breath. "No, that's not the truth," you say. Then you tell them the truth: that your curiosity led you to the abandoned fort. They listen in stony silence until you've finished.

"And you, Og. You went with your friend of your own free will?" asks one of the elders.

"Yes, Venerable One. I was as curious as my friend," Og admits.

The elders confer for a few minutes, and then the oldest member addresses you. "You are both brave, resourceful, and bright. But we worry that your curiosity will prevent you from adjusting to normal Orcan life. We have therefore decided to send you both to the planet of curiosity—Earth."

Turn to page 25.

36

"Yes, I was alone," you say. "I didn't know that Fort Triumphant was forbidden or that it was in the Lost Region." You say this with difficulty, since you're not used to lying.

The Supreme Senate confers for several minutes. Then the leader speaks again. "Your body and mind are vessels for excessive curiosity. The best cure for you is a trip to Earth—the planet of curiosity."

You turn and look at your friend. Og seems about to speak. You shake your head, warning Og to remain quiet.

But Og doesn't seem to understand you.

"I went there, too," Og shouts. "I went to Fort Triumphant!"

Turn to page 63.

"I guess it's better to be introduced to one of their governments," you say. "But why is there more than one?"

There's a burst of laughter in the great hall.

"It is a young planet," the oldest elder tells you and Og. "Its people are fighting all the time. They do not trust each other, so be wary of whom you trust. They never agree on anything, so one government is not enough. Neither are two, nor a hundred. Earth's political system is a haphazard mishmash.

"Unless you two set them straight, the Earthlings may blow themselves out of their universe."

You feel a sense of mission, of importance, of destiny. You risk asking another question.

"What are their problems? Isn't there enough food? Is it an impoverished planet? Is that their problem?"

"No. It is a planet rich in everything. There is enough, more than enough. They just do not share. They are like little children squabbling over toys. Only *their* toys can kill."

Turn to page 28.

You're in scattered clouds, twenty-six thousand feet above ground when your ship is surrounded by Chinese fighter ships. You notice that they're old-fashioned crafts, with wings, but they still look powerful.

Suddenly you receive a transmission: "Identify yourselves. Repeat, identify yourselves." The voice barks over your radio.

"Friendlies," you transmit back on the same frequency. "From the planet Orca in the Heraclean System."

More aircraft join the original fighters. They circle you in graceful, slow arcs.

"Follow us. Do not make any hostile or unplanned moves. We wish to believe you."

The descent through the clouds is brief, and you emerge over a rolling, treeless terrain dotted with small villages. It's agricultural land. The fighters direct you to a military base with a landing field.

"Looks okay to me," Og says hopefully.

"I hope so," you reply uncertainly.

Turn to page 33.

As soon as your spacecraft reaches beyond Orca's gravitational pull, you get to work checking the ship's computer library on Earth history. You're amazed at the number of different places you have to choose from as a landing site.

"How can we decide?" Og moans. "There are too many countries."

"Let's go for one of the biggest. Or the most powerful," you say.

"Okay," Og agrees. "This place called China looks pretty big. We could try landing there. Or how about this one—the U.S.A.? They call themselves a superpower," he says.

You have to decide quickly. Your uneventful voyage has been so swift you're almost entering Earth's atmosphere.

If you decide to land in China,
turn to page 51.

If you decide to go to the U.S.A.,
turn to page 69.

"I cannot give up my curiosity," you say. "Just as I cannot stop breathing. I'm sorry that this displeases you."

The leader of the Supreme Senate turns to you and speaks in a faint whisper. "Tell us. Why are you so curious?"

"Aren't all young people?" you ask.

"Has anyone led you astray?"

"No, no one."

"Have you been in touch with other beings?"

"You mean from other planets? No."

"Have you been reading any strange books?"

"No, only what's allowed, what's in the library."

"Have you gone exploring in the Way Far Back?"

"Yes. With my friends. We like the Way Far Back."

"And did you go beyond, into the Lost Region?"

"Well . . ."

"It is simple. Yes or no? Did you or did you not enter the Lost Region?"

You glance at Og, then at the elders.

If you say yes, turn to page 22.

If you say no, turn to page 35.

"Run for it!" yells Og.

"Head for the trees," you cry as you and Og race each other to the nearest Juwawa tree.

You reach the tree inches ahead of the lizard and quickly climb up.

"I hope it's not a tree climber," you say to Og as the two of you reach the nearest branches. You and Og turn and look down. The lizard is lying by the roots of the tree with its tongue darting in and out and its yellow eyes blinking.

"I don't think it is," says Og. "But it doesn't look in a hurry to go anyplace else, either."

The lizard's eyes watch your every move.

"If it stays there, we'll be stuck up here until a park ranger finds us," you say to Og. "And I don't even know if the park rangers patrol the Lost Region. It's not something I've ever been curious about," you add mournfully.

The End

"Okay. Let's go," you reply.

You signal your ship and are lifted up into the spacecraft by the ascender beam. The hatch closes immediately behind you.

Peering through a viewing port, you see a look of surprise on the face of the Chinese leader. He's so stunned, he's still holding out his hand. The troops surrounding him are aiming their weapons at you.

"Hit the rapid-altitude button!" you yell.

Og presses the RAB. With a groan, the spacecraft soars away from this part of Earth. In seconds, you easily outdistance the Chinese fighter craft chasing you.

You and Og sit at your ship's linguistic computer, listening to the Chinese.

"What did we do wrong?" you hear the leader ask. "We offered them peace, but they didn't trust us."

When you hear that, you groan. "Og, we've made a big mistake," you say.

Turn to page 74.

When your foot hits the pedal, the engine shuts down immediately. And with the g-force no longer pinning you against your seat, you can reach the manual controls. You press buttons as quickly as you can, and Og hits the auxiliary power supply. The ship's nose slowly turns upward and the spaceship starts to climb.

When the spaceship is safely under control, you put it back on autopilot and let the computer set the course for Earth.

Turn to page 53.

As you draw closer to Washington D.C., the airspace below you begins to fill with craft that you recognize as ancient fighter jets. You maneuver your spaceship, aiming it at a large open space near a needlelike projection in the middle of the city.

At the same time you push a button on your computer console. A message of friendship is broadcast on all light and sound waves.

You descend to two hundred feet and stop. The air around you is cluttered with buglike flying machines. Above you fly the squadrons of winged aircraft. On the ground, hundreds of people dressed in uniforms are waiting for you.

Turn to page 27.

You remember from your briefing by the elders that the inhabitants of Earth love television.

But before you can answer the leader's question, two rockets strike thirty yards from your group. The wiry men fling themselves onto the ground, then look in the direction of the attack. You see pinpricks of light that turn into zinging metal objects zipping past your head. You and Og drop to the ground, too.

As quickly as it started, the attack is over.

"You, reporter, you come with us, no?" the leader says, grinning. "We show you something."

If you consider pretending to be a TV reporter, turn to page 73.

If you try to return to the spaceship, turn to page 95.

Your craft fills the sky and floods the ground with golden light. The crowd below gasps. Some run in terror, fleeing in cars and buses. Others stay, waiting for you and Og to emerge from the spaceship.

Slowly and majestically, you and Og glide one hundred feet down the descender beam to the top of the pyramid.

The crowd utters a collective "Ohhh," as the two of you begin to descend the steep stairs of the pyramid. That's when you realize you forgot one thing . . .

Turn to page 87.

You and Og control the spaceship as best you can as you guide it back to Orca.

"Let's head for the sea," you say. "If we crash into the water, we have a better chance to survive."

You manage to head the ship in the direction of the sea. As the spaceship loses power, it flys over the surface. Frantically you press several buttons on the control console and, at the last second, the spaceship skims the surface, crashing through the waves. Finally the ship stops, still afloat.

You and Og are soon rescued by the Orcan Coast Guard.

The End

"China it is," Og says, agreeing with your choice. "And just in time. We're entering Earth's atmosphere." Og fiddles with the directional navigator.

"The thing that interests me about China is its history," you say. "It's an old culture, at least in Earth terms."

"So, big deal. It's old. What's that got to do with us?" Og asks.

"I think an older culture that's seen it all—wars, revolutions, success, famine—would be more receptive to our message."

"And just what *is* our message?" Og asks.

Turn to page 70.

Finally, you enter Earth's atmosphere. Your spaceship descends in a slow arc, and then hovers above a beautiful stone pyramid in the midst of a scrubby jungle.

"This is Mexico," Og tells you, reading from the computer display. "And we're over one of the ancient pyramids of the Mayan people. It's called Chichén Itzá. Shall we descend now, or wait for dark?"

*If you want to descend immediately,
turn to page 66.*

*If you want to wait for nightfall,
turn to page 62.*

"No, I wasn't alone," you blurt out. "Og was with me."

Og comes forward and takes your hand in a symbol of friendship.

"We didn't plan this," you tell the elders. "It simply happened. Curiosity isn't so bad. When you're curious, you wonder. When you wonder, you explore. When you explore, you discover. We're stronger for the experience."

The elders smile at you and Og with benign expressions on their faces.

"Your hearts are in the right place, but your bodies are not. Orcan society is an old and civilized society. We prefer to remain tranquil. We keep our young population to a minimum because young people are always so curious. Too much curiosity overexcites us, and we guard against this. Yet, we understand your feelings; all of us were young once . . . many years ago."

The hushed chamber is electric with emotion. "For the good of us all, you must travel to Earth— the planet of curiosity. You will stay there until your curiosity is satisfied! You might even do the Earthlings some good."

The leader of the Supreme Senate turns to you. "We could send you as official diplomats," she says, "but under the circumstances, I think an unofficial visit would be preferable."

Turn to page 16.

Aboard your ship the Earthlings are anxious but not frightened. There is a moment of awkward silence.

"Many of us on Earth have hoped for contact with life from another planet," the woman begins. "Things are happening so fast on our planet that we need your help." She pauses and looks at you and Og anxiously. "Can you help us?"

"We'll try," you respond together.

"Then, welcome," she says warmly.

"We're glad to be here," you say enthusiastically. "We're curious to learn more about your planet."

"I'm curious, too," says the young man. "Who are you?"

You and Og smile. "We're Orcans," you say. "I guess you could say we're the first Orcan ambassadors to Earth."

The End

One grinning guerrilla offers you a weapon, holding it out proudly as though it were the finest gift in the world.

You shake your head, not wanting anything to do with weapons.

"Where is TV camera?" asks another man.

Some of the guerrillas are leaning casually against the spacecraft. They show no interest in it.

"Have you ever seen one of these things before?" you ask, pointing to the spaceship.

Turn to page 23.

The people in uniforms point pieces of long hollow metal at you. You hear popping sounds, and watch as small, sharp-pointed metal zip by.

You and Og smile at this strange method of greeting. Then, one of the sharp-pointed metal pieces slams into Og, and Og tumbles off the descender beam. Before you can react, three of the metal pieces strike you. As you crash to Earth, you hear a voice say, "I'm sure my bullets got both of them."

Bullets? You've never heard of them. What are bullets? you wonder. It's the last question you ever ask.

The End

Your spaceship begins its descent. According to the computer display, you'll land in a Tibetan settlement on the outskirts of a town in the mountain kingdom of Nepal. The town is called Pokhara, and it sits at the foot of the Annapurna range of mountains.

You bring the spaceship down carefully, landing just beyond the courtyard of a Buddhist temple.

You and Og step out of the spaceship and listen.

Om mane padme hum.

A man comes forward. He bows to you and Og, his hands clasped together, fingers pointing to his forehead.

Turn to page 100.

The woman and the crowd watch you silently.
You reach out your hand toward hers.
After a moment—she touches you.
You and the crowd are enveloped by a white aura. Everywhere, there is silence.
"Who are you?" you ask.
"Just me," she replies. "A believer."
"In what?" you ask.
"Hope," is her simple answer.
The strength of her belief convinces you that this ancient site is a good place to begin your exploration of Earth and its peoples.

The End

"Night is better for Orcans. Let's wait," you say. "And we can get some sleep while the ship hovers."

"Fine with me," Og agrees.

The spacecraft hovers unseen above the Earth as you sleep.

You're asleep for only a few hours when your alarm system is activated.

Og jumps up and points out the viewing port. "That stupid computer! It landed the spaceship while we were asleep."

Another alarm goes off, interrupting your thoughts. A life-form is on board your spacecraft and it's *not* Orcan!

Your spacecraft is equipped with a self-defense system, but it's not automatic—someone has to activate it. But should you activate it without knowing what life-form has intruded into your ship?

If you decide to wait, turn to page 72.

If you decide to activate the defense mechanism, turn to page 83.

The Supreme Senate huddles in conference. Then the leader speaks again. "You, Og, must go with your friend," she says. "The Senate wishes you both a speedy recovery. You may return to Orca when your curiosity has been sated."

The two of you are led out of the chamber and marched to the transit port. There you're given space suits—loose-fitting, comfortable, and functional—and assigned to a drone survey ship which is preparing for a close-range Earth reconnaissance mission.

Og smiles at you and gives you the traditional open-hand signal for good luck.

The craft is cleared for departure.

Turn to page 92.

"What's plan B?" you ask Og anxiously. "The computer isn't working."

"Return to Orca as fast as we can!" Og replies instantly.

"Not yet," you say.

In frustration you kick the computer. It rumbles, vibrates, and sparks to life. When its lights blink on, you activate the self-defense mechanism.

READY TO REPEL INVADERS. WHAT LEVEL OF FORCE IS REQUIRED?

"Medium force," you keyboard.

WHAT RADIUS?

If you want to limit the defensive force to just the spacecraft, turn to page 98.

If you consider extending the defensive force, turn to page 102.

"Let's descend now," you say. "I'm too curious to wait."

"Look at all those people down there," exclaims Og, pointing at the huge crowd gathered at the base of the pyramid.

You ask the computer for more information, and read it aloud to Og. "It says here that Chichén Itzá was the center of the Mayan culture, hundreds of years ago. Now, people come from all over the world to see these pyramids. They're curious, just as we are!"

"Let me see," says Og, turning toward the display terminal. "The Mayans disappeared," Og reads, "but they left behind this magnificent, deserted, ceremonial site." You and Og admire the huge pyramid with its stone steps leading to a platform at the top.

"It also says that the Mayans predicted the arrival of beings from outer space. That's us!" Og declares proudly.

"Uh, Og," you interrupt your friend. "I don't think *these* people are expecting us," you say as you lower your spacecraft to within one hundred feet of the pyramid.

Turn to page 49.

"They won't hurt us, Og. Come on." You tug at your friend's sleeve.

"You go first," Og replies.

"All right." You walk forward, with your arm outstretched, and grasp the hand of the Chinese officer. "We are from the planet Orca, and we're happy to see you. Please accept this as a symbol of our friendship."

You reach into your pocket, but you don't find what you're looking for. You turn to Og and whisper frantically, "Where is the box? What did we do with the gift?"

"Oh, that." Og hurriedly searches his pockets. He breathes a sigh of relief as he pulls the box from his pocket and hands it to you. You open the box and remove an Orcan crystal. It's a little smaller than a baseball, perfect in shape and form.

"This crystal is a token of our friendship." You hand the crystal to the Chinese officer. "Orcans have watched your planet for centuries. Perhaps we can help in these dangerous times."

The officer stares at the crystal, then passes it around. You hear murmurs of awe and appreciation.

Turn to page 34.

You give a quick command to your space computer, and your spacecraft speeds into space to await your next command.

You and Og are alone on Earth.

"I hope you know what you're doing," Og says.

"Not really," you reply.

You walk down the remaining steps until you're standing in front of the Earth woman.

Turn to page 61.

"The U.S.A.," you tell Og. "The computer tapes say it's a young, aggressive, and idealistic country. But I've also heard it's always in trouble," you add.

"Maybe there are too many problems to solve," Og suggests.

"Well, let's have a look."

You and Og guide your spacecraft to within a mile of the Earth's surface. You crisscross the country at megasonic speed, from San Francisco to New York City, Detroit to Dallas.

"It looks a lot like Orca," Og comments.

"It does. I didn't expect that."

Finally, you end up over Washington, D.C. Your computer briefing had pointed Washington out as the center of government, although it indicated New York City as a formidable power base as well.

You set your controls for a slow descent to Earth.

Turn to page 46.

That catches you unaware. Now that you think about it, you aren't really certain what the Supreme Orcan Senate wants you to achieve on Earth. Peace? Harmony? Is that what Orca is about? you ask yourself. Maybe all Earthlings need is time; time will lead to peace and harmony. But you wonder if Earth has enough time.

"I don't know, Og. I guess we'll just have to play it as it comes."

"Well, we'd better start playing pretty soon. We're in Chinese airspace and they know it!" Og exclaims.

Turn to page 39.

72

You and Og wait quietly, watching the computer display. Suddenly, the computer pinpoints the location of the intruder. ZONE E flashes on the display.

"Let's go, Og," you say.

"Not me," Og answers. "You go. I'll stay here as backup in case you get into trouble."

You don't blame Og for being scared, but you need to know what's back in zone E.

With your courage rapidly fading, you leave the safety of the passenger zone and, unarmed, head for your fate.

Turn to page 106.

You look at the guerrillas waving their weapons in the air and crying war slogans. You and Og feel uneasy with these men. On Orca, violence hasn't been used in thousands of years. But if you say you're not TV reporters, they may try to harm you and Og. You decide to play along with them until you can devise an escape strategy.

"Yes, sure. Television reporters," you reply.

"Good! You give us good publicity, we give you gifts," says the leader.

You nervously glance at Og. But Og just shrugs. It's up to you.

Turn to page 56.

"What mistake?" Og asks.

"On Orca we're raised to trust and believe one another. Orcans have outgrown most other planets because we trust one another as a way of life. The elders told us that civilizations on Earth are not automatically to be trusted, because Earthlings don't trust each other."

"So?" Og says.

"The Chinese were trying to welcome us, and we didn't trust them. If we don't trust them, why should they trust us?" You look at Og to see if he understands. He smiles back at you knowingly.

"All right" he says. "Let's try again someplace else."

"And this time," you say, "we'll give those Earthlings the benefit of the doubt."

The End

You and Og wake up from what felt like a short nap to find that the computer has already landed the spaceship on Earth.

Cautiously, you step outside your spacecraft. Stretching and yawning, you sniff the air. It seems okay. The gravity of Earth is a little less strong than that of Orca, but you'll adjust to it.

"Strange place. No people around here," Og comments as he does some calisthenics to unkink his cramped muscles.

Turn to page 80.

"The computer says Taos is an ancient Indian pueblo village," Og tells you as your ship heads for New Mexico. "It's known for its community living."

"I'm going to descend slowly, Og. We don't want to scare anyone. Put on the sound receiver. Let's listen to the chanting."

"Will do," Og replies, adjusting the spaceship's sensitive sound-detection devices.

The cabin of the spaceship fills with a rhythmic, pulsing vibration. It sounds wonderful, energizing, and powerful to you.

Hummm. Hummm. Hummm.

The spaceship descends slowly, glowing in the setting sun. Peering out the viewing ports, you see desert and mountains and a few winking lights from a town.

Now you're one hundred feet above the chanting. You slow the descent, and the ship hovers in the air.

"Aren't we going to join them?" Og asks.

You nod and lower the spaceship gently to Earth.

You open the hatch and step out.

Turn to page 97.

You strain to reach the manual controls but the g-force is too powerful. Your arm is pinned back to you as if your body were a magnet.

The spaceship levels off, then the nose begins to point down. You're hurtling back to Orca! If you don't take fast action, you and Og will perish in a ball of fire.

You hear a voice coming through your helmet's radio. Og is trying to tell you something, but your helmet is vibrating so violently that you can't understand the words. Og points frantically at your feet.

You look down and see a pedal. But what does it do? you wonder.

If you step on the pedal, turn to page 45.

If you hesitate, trying to think of something else to do, turn to page 85.

You and Og pass the time reading the computer's library of adventure stories. After awhile you become bored.

"Let's see what the computer has to say about our mission," you suggest.

You keyboard a request for information about your mission to Earth. You're astounded by what you find.

"I can't believe this," you say. "I thought we were being sent to Earth, but the computer has us programmed to land on Ocrania."

Turn to page 111.

Suddenly you're surrounded by a band of wiry, bearded, heavily armed, and poorly dressed men with turbans wrapped around their heads. They're pointing archaic looking weapons at you and Og.

"Russki?" the leader says.

"No," you reply.

"Americanski?"

"No."

"TV reporter?" is his third guess. He looks at you eagerly, licking his chapped lips.

Turn to page 48.

"We would feel more comfortable in our spacecraft," you explain to the woman. "Would you like to see it, and speak to us there?"

"All right," she replies.

"Can I come, too?" asks a young man.

"Of course," Og replies.

"Anyone else care to come on board?" you ask the crowd.

No one moves, and there's a mumbling of voices. Finally a man steps forward.

"My name's Becker. I'll go with you."

"Good. Follow us," you reply.

You and Og lead the way up the steps of the pyramid.

"They seem to trust us," Og whispers to you.

"Why shouldn't they?" you remark, as you activate the ascender beam, and the five of you are transported up to the spaceship.

Turn to page 55.

"We'll have to use force to get rid of the intruders," you say.

"Force can be useful, but it can result in more force," Og points out.

"We'll just repel the intruders. We won't harm them."

"How do you know that? You've never done this before. You might use too much force," Og argues.

"It's a chance we must take, Og. We have to defend ourselves. And our ship."

Og turns away from you, mumbling Orcan phrases of discontent as you prepare to repel the invaders. You program the spacecraft computer for self-defense, but it doesn't respond.

Turn to page 65.

It doesn't take long for your ship to reach the Himalayan mountains, a jagged range of snow-covered peaks that rises over five miles into the sky and runs almost two thousand miles from Afghanistan to the farthest reaches of India.

"Og, can you trace the chanting sound?" you ask.

"Yes, but it's difficult. There are so many mountains in the way."

Your ship is cruising so low you can almost touch the tops of the gigantic mountains. They glisten in the morning sun, alluring and dangerous at the same time.

"Wait. Okay, I've got it," Og says.

Turn to page 59.

That pedal could be for anything, you think to yourself. Stepping on it might even cause you and Og to be ejected into outer space. And that's the last thing you need.

But you've got to try something!

Suddenly, all is quiet. "The booster rockets must have shut down," Og says, breathing a sigh of relief. "We're running on the main engine again." Og gives you the thumbs-up sign.

"Let's not get too confident," you tell your friend. "We're not out of this yet."

Turn to page 94.

You didn't diminish your aura energy! You and Og are surrounded by a visible field—a glowing mixture of white and orange light. But it's too late now to do anything about it.

You walk halfway down the steps. "We bring peace and friendship," you quote from the phrasetape the elders gave you when you left Orca. "We have journeyed to reach you. We wish to be of help to your world."

The people stare at you as if hypnotized. You hope the elders knew what they were doing when they sent you and Og to Earth. The people here don't seem at all receptive to your message.

Og looks nervously at you, waiting for some response.

"Do not be afraid. We come on a mission of peace," you add.

A woman steps forward from the mass of people surrounding the base of the pyramid. "If you speak the truth, send away your spacecraft and meet with us."

If you do what she suggests, turn to page 68.

If you ask to meet with her on board your spacecraft, turn to page 82.

Og gives you the thumbs-up sign and you both eject. You free-fall for as long as you can, before pulling the ripcords on your parachutes.

Steam rises off your hot space suits as you descend through the cool Orcan atmosphere.

You and Og land with a jolt and are blown by the wind until you manage to cut the cords of your parachutes. You sit for a moment to catch your breath.

"I wonder where we are," you say to Og.

Og stands up and looks around. "You're not going to believe this," Og says, smiling from ear to ear, pointing to a clearing a hundred yards away. "But look over there."

You get to your feet and look in the direction that Og is pointing. You and Og start laughing.

"Fort Triumphant!" you say in unison.

The End

Quickly you press buttons on the control console. The ship lurches left and narrowly misses the satellite. You set the spaceship on autocontrol and head in the direction of Earth.

"We may as well try to get some sleep," Og says to you.

"I don't know if that's a good idea," you reply. "The way this spaceship is malfunctioning, I don't trust the computer to get us to Earth."

If you go to sleep, turn to page 76.

If you stay awake, turn to page 79.

You maneuver the ship, trying to position it so that the ship's docking arm can hook onto the approaching satellite. But you're traveling too fast.

You feel the jolt as your spaceship collides with the satellite, and spins out of control.

You and Og fight to regain control, but the spinning is making you dizzy. You feel yourself starting to black out.

You try to reach the ship's autocontrol button, but you don't know if you can remain conscious long enough.

You feel Og's hand next to yours, and together you're able to push the button. The ship's autocontrol takes over and the spinning stops.

You look at the navigational indicator. Something is very wrong.

"According to the indicator, we're supposed to be heading into outer space," you say to Og. "But I can see the surface of Orca getting larger."

Og looks out a viewing port.

"Either the autonavigator is still haywire or the satellite damaged the navigational equipment," you say. "We'll have to try and steer the spaceship manually. Again!"

Turn to page 107.

ARMING DEFENSIVE WEAPONS.
READY AT YOUR SIGNAL.

You read the display message and keyboard, "Now!"

The computer relays a signal to the defensive weapons and a beam of energy designed to negate hostile action is sent out.

The beam is a soft purple ray of light that emits a low, rumbling hum. When viewed from a distance by inhabitants of Earth, the beam pulsates like a blinker or a signal light.

"Look!" says Og, standing at one of the viewing ports.

Turn to page 105.

You and Og check your space suits and engage your seat restraints. The space-traffic controller clears your craft for blast-off.

The spaceship rumbles and takes off so quickly that you and Og are thrown back against your seats.

You look out the viewing ports and watch Orca, and home, slowly slip away. This is the first time either of you has gone beyond the atmosphere of Orca.

Suddenly the booster rockets kick in and the spaceship vibrates violently. A red warning light flashes on the control panel.

"What's wrong?" Og asks. You can see panic in your friend's eyes.

"I don't know," you respond as calmly as you can. You quickly spot the trouble: the auto-navigator has gone haywire. You'll have to pilot the spaceship manually or you'll crash back to Orca!

Turn to page 78.

With the g-force lessened, you and Og can reach the manual controls. You press buttons on the console, trying to get the spaceship to break out of Orca's gravitational pull. You manage to point the ship's nose upward, but without the booster rockets there's not enough power to escape the Orcan atmosphere.

"We'll have to reactivate the booster rockets," Og says.

"They've already used up a lot of fuel. What if we don't have enough left to make it all the way to Earth?" you argue. "We could get stranded in outer space."

"That's true," agrees Og. "So what should we do?"

If you try to reactivate the booster rockets, turn to page 108.

If you try to get back to Orca, turn to page 50.

"Let's get back inside the ship," you whisper to Og.

You mumble something about equipment, and you and Og are back in the spaceship before the guerrillas can do anything to stop you.

"Full power for lift-off," you say in as calm a voice as possible.

"Full power," Og confirms. Your spaceship rises upward in a smooth, noiseless path.

"Altitude three thousand feet and climbing," Og says. "Altitude ten thousand feet. Altitude thirty thousand feet and steady. What course?"

"Let's cruise around and observe," you answer. "Somewhere, we'll find a better place to land. All the inhabitants of Earth can't be violent."

Slowly orbiting the Earth, you pick up two readings that seem promising. From a place called Taos, in the state of New Mexico in the U.S.A., you pick up sound vibrations of music and chanting.

The other positive reading is from a mountain village in the Himalayan range. Similar chanting is coming from there.

If you decide to go to Taos, New Mexico,
turn to page 77.

If you decide to descend in the Himalayas,
turn to page 84.

A circle of people look at you as you step down. Their faces are open and trusting. You see no fear, only welcome in their eyes. One comes forward. He's old, wrinkled, and stooped.

"Welcome," he says. "May Earth be your home. May these people be your people."

You take his hand in yours, feeling the love of the people for all things that move on Earth and in the cosmos, for the past, present, and future. You sense hope and joy in the people, and you feel it in yourself.

"Og, this is a better place than I expected," you say.

Og, shaking the old man's hand, nods in agreement.

"Earth is more than a planet of curiosity," you say, smiling—"it's a planet of hope as well."

The End

You keyboard a reply.

ZONE ADJUSTED. TIME OF ACTION REQUIRED?

"Wait!" you reply.

You try to imagine the life-form that may be invading your territory. Orcans are trained to place their minds into a certain mind-set that allows them to see alien life-forms to a high degree of accuracy.

But this time, no matter how hard you try, you can't bring an image into focus.

"Something is blocking me," you say to Og. "I can't get an image of this thing."

"You're blocking yourself, with fear or anger," Og replies.

"Well, if you're so fearless, you try," you say.

"Okay," Og says confidently.

Turn to page 103.

"What's that, Og?" you ask.

"Sounds like visitors," he replies.

"Hey, let us in!" "We're friendly!" several voices call from outside the spaceship.

"Do we trust them?" Og asks you.

You hesitate and think about the danger that may await you outside. But then your curiosity gets the better of you.

"There's only one way to find out," you say. "Open the hatch."

Turn to page 112.

"Na maste," the man says. "Welcome, I am Chodak. You have come at the right time. The world is in need of wisdom from other planets. You shall help us with our problems. You are welcome here."

Chodak claps his hands three times, and great horns, cymbals, and drums begin a ceremony of thanksgiving and welcome.

You and Og smile at each other. You know now you can be of great help to the planet Earth.

The End

You look at Og and ask, "How wide a radius should I request?" From the viewing port of your spaceship, Earth appears mysterious and over-whelming. You find your curiosity is slowly being overpowered by your fear of unknown Earth dangers.

Og shrugs in answer to your question, indicating the choice is yours.

You turn from the computer and begin to pace the passenger zone.

"Orcans are known for their fearlessness," encourages Og.

"But there's so little to fear on Orca," you reply. "No weapons, no violence. We *must* protect ourselves. Remember the other Orcans? The ones who never returned from voyages to Earth?"

"Okay, okay. Let's do it," Og says.

You program a wide radius and activate the defensive force.

Turn to page 91.

Og gets into the proper mind-set and goes to work. His face wrinkles; the muscles tighten. Og leans backward, his head touching the floor.

"It must be a *really* strong mind at work. It's blocking me, too."

The computer blinks on: ALL ZONES SAFE.

"What was it?" you wonder aloud, but before you can ask the computer, it shuts itself off.

"Well, Og, we'll just wait for dawn and see what happens on Earth."

The two of you fall into a deep, dreamless sleep, almost a trance. Finally, you're wakened by a gentle knocking sound.

Turn to page 99.

People are being drawn to the spaceship by the comforting light and the gentle sound. They're not armed. They're coming in peace.

The sun is rising in the east. Day has brought Og and you freedom from fear. You descend from your spacecraft and are warmly welcomed to Earth.

"Not bad," you say to Og, as a young child hands you a bunch of flowers and quickly kisses your cheek. "Who knows? Maybe we'll like this planet Earth so much we won't return to Orca, either."

The End

The door to zone E is slightly ajar. Dim red lights illuminate the supplies that were put aboard the survey ship for you and Og.

You edge inside the bay, flattening yourself against the side walls. Slowly you inch forward.

You hear a slight noise and feel a rush of air in front of your feet. You look down and see a small, furry creature. Its eyes gleam. It has sharp teeth. It stands on four legs.

You back away as the creature screeches. You manage to back out the door and retreat to the passenger zone.

"Well, what was it?" Og asks.

Turn to page 31.

You depress the manual control button and keyboard commands into the computer. But your actions have no effect on the steering of the ship.

"I think more than just the navigational equipment got damaged," you say. "We can't even steer the ship."

"Looks like we're headed back to Orca," Og says.

The spaceship breaks back through Orca's atmosphere and plummets toward the planet's surface.

"It's getting pretty warm," Og says, tugging at his space suit. "Don't you think?"

"The protective shield must have been damaged, too," you answer.

"If it was," Og says nervously, "we'll never reach Orca alive. We'll burn to death."

Turn to page 110.

108

You press the button to reactivate the booster rockets. The ship's nose points upward. You call for full power and again the spaceship shudders. But this time it remains on course as it strains to break free of Orca's gravitational grip.

With one last shudder, the ship breaks through the Orcan atmosphere into outer space.

"That was a close one," you say to Og.

"I have a funny feeling it won't be the last close call we have on this trip," Og answers, pointing out a viewing port.

Looming in front of you is an Orcan satellite, and it's heading right for you!

"If we can hook up to the satellite, maybe we can be rescued," Og says quickly. "But then we'll never get to see Earth," Og adds softly.

If you try to hook up to the satellite,
turn to page 90.

If you try to avoid hitting the satellite,
turn to page 89.

The inside of the spaceship begins to get incredibly hot. Even through your protective space suits, you feel the intense, ovenlike heat.

"I've got an idea," Og says. "Let's activate the emergency ejection seats and bail out."

"We can't eject now," you say. "The air's too thin up here. We won't be able to breathe." You feel the heat penetrating your space suit. In a few more minutes it will be unbearable.

"We can't wait much longer, either," says Og.

"You're right," you reply. "We'll have to take a chance and eject—and hope we have enough air in our suits to breath until we reach the surface."

Turn to page 88.

"But Ocrania's barely habitable!" Og says.

"I thought it was only used to mine ore for Orca," you reply.

"Then that means"—Og looks at you in disbelief—"that we're being sent to Ocrania as miners."

"Slave labor is a better term for it," you say. "It's lucky we didn't go to sleep. Let's put the spaceship back on manual control and head for Earth."

"I hope the people of Earth are more trustworthy than the Orcan elders," Og says.

You and Og take over control of the spaceship and fly to Earth, where countless adventures await you on the planet of curiosity.

The End

Og opens the hatch door.

At the entrance, on the steps of the Mayan pyramid, and all around its base, a large, silent crowd stares up at you. You hesitate. Then you and Og step out of the spaceship.

The crowd claps, cheers, and shouts "Welcome!"

You smile at Og. You're going to enjoy your time on Earth.

The End

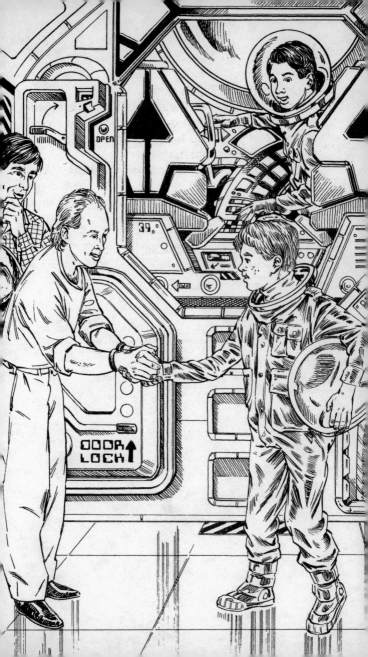

ABOUT THE AUTHOR

R.A. MONTGOMERY is an educator and publisher. A graduate of Williams College, he also studied in graduate programs at Yale University and New York University. After serving in a variety of administrative capacities at Williston Academy and Columbia University, he co-founded Waitsfield Summer School in 1965. Following that, Montgomery helped found a research and development firm specializing in the development of educational programs. He worked for several years as a consultant to the Peace Corps in Washington, D.C., and West Africa. He is now both a writer and a publisher.

ABOUT THE ILLUSTRATOR

FRANK BOLLE studied at Pratt Institute. He has worked as an illustrator for many national magazines and now creates and draws cartoons for magazines as well. He has also worked in advertising and children's educational materials and has drawn and collaborated on several newspaper comic strips, including *Annie*. A native of Brooklyn Heights, New York, Mr. Bolle now works and lives in Westport, Connecticut.

CHOOSE YOUR OWN ADVENTURE®

☐	25764 TREASURE DIVER #32	$2.25
☐	25918 THE DRAGON'S DEN #33	$2.25
☐	24344 THE MYSTERY OF HIGHLAND CREST #34	$1.95
☐	25961 JOURNEY TO STONEHENGE #35	$2.25
☐	24522 THE SECRET TREASURE OF TIBET #36	$1.95
☐	25778 WAR WITH THE EVIL POWER MASTER #37	$2.25
☐	25818 SUPERCOMPUTER #39	$2.25
☐	26265 THE THRONE OF ZEUS #40	$2.25
☐	26062 SEARCH FOR MOUNTAIN GORILLAS #41	$2.25
☐	26313 THE MYSTERY OF ECHO LODGE #42	$2.25
☐	26522 GRAND CANYON ODYSSEY #43	$2.25
☐	24892 THE MYSTERY OF URA SENKE #44	$1.95
☐	26386 YOU ARE A SHARK #45	$2.25
☐	24991 THE DEADLY SHADOW #46	$1.95
☐	26388 OUTLAWS OF SHERWOOD FOREST #47	$2.25
☐	25134 SPY FOR GEORGE WASHINGTON #48	$1.95
☐	25177 DANGER AT ANCHOR MINE #49	$1.95
☐	25296 RETURN TO THE CAVE OF TIME #50	$1.95
☐	25242 MAGIC OF THE UNICORN #51	$2.25
☐	25488 GHOST HUNTER #52	$2.25
☐	25489 CASE OF THE SILK KING #53	$2.25
☐	25490 FOREST OF FEAR #54	$2.25
☐	25491 TRUMPET OF TERROR #55	$2.25
☐	25861 ENCHANTED KINGDOM #56	$2.25
☐	25741 THE ANTIMATTER FORMULA #57	$2.25
☐	25813 STATUE OF LIBERTY ADVENTURE #58	$2.25
☐	25885 TERROR ISLAND #59	$2.25
☐	25941 VANISHED! #60	$2.25
☐	27890 BEYOND ESCAPE! #61	$2.50
☐	26040 SUGARCANE ISLAND #62	$2.25
☐	27694 MYSTERY OF THE SECRET ROOM #63	$2.50
☐	26197 VOLCANO #64	$2.25
☐	27695 MARDI GRAS MYSTERY #65	$2.50
☐	26484 THE SECRET OF NINJA #66	$2.25
☐	27696 SEASIDE MYSTERY #67	$2.50
☐	27698 SECRET OF THE SUN GOD #68	$2.50
☐	27697 ROCK & ROLL MYSTERY #69	$2.50
☐	26669 INVADERS OF THE PLANET EARTH #70	$2.50
☐	26723 SPACE VAMPIRE #71	$2.50
☐	26983 GHOST HUNTER #72	$2.50
☐	26725 BEYOND THE GREAT WALL #73	$2.50
☐	26904 LONGHORN TERRITORY #74	$2.50
☐	26887 PLANET OF DRAGONS #75	$2.50
☐	27004 THE MONA LISA IS MISSING #76	$2.50
☐	27063 THE FIRST OLYMPICS #77	$2.50
☐	27123 RETURN TO ATLANTIS #78	$2.50
☐	26950 MYSTERY OF THE SACRED STONES #79	$2.50

Prices and availability subject to change without notice.

- -

Special Offer
Buy a Bantam Book
for only 50¢.

Now you can order the exciting books you've
been wanting to read straight from Bantam's
latest catalog of hundreds of titles. *And* this
special offer gives you the opportunity to purchase
a Bantam book for only 50¢. Here's how:

By ordering any five books at the regular
price per order, you can also choose any other
single book listed (up to a $5.95 value) for only
50¢. Some restrictions do apply, so for further
details send for Bantam's catalog of titles today.

Just send us your name and address and
we'll send you Bantam Book's SHOP AT
HOME CATALOG!

This Book
Donated By:

Friends of the Library
Scobey, MT 59263